Want a free Ebook? Join my mailing list to get my monthly newsletter!

Cover Design by Covergirl Design

 Created with Vellum

GILDED CAGE

MATILDA MARTEL
MIA BARRETT

PROLOGUE

EVE

Something's coming.

My grandmother used to say I had a third eye, a knack for clairvoyance and strange premonitions. When I was seven, I had a feeling the last time I saw my grandfather would be the last time I saw my grandfather. As we left his house after our Sunday visit, I ran back in to say goodbye a second time.

He died in his sleep later that night.

I've avoided three car accidents by refusing to get in someone's car and I've tried to talk girlfriends from going out with men who eventually cheated on them. None listened to me, but they can't say they weren't warned. My intuition isn't consistent and it isn't a slam dunk. But tonight's the exception. I can feel something is just around the corner.

This time, it's undeniable.

I run my palm along my forehead then slide it down my cheeks. My flushed face warms my trembling hand as beads of sweat gather at my temples. I pretend to brush a few messy strands of hair and wipe away the evidence. This is no time to panic or overreact. It's girls' night.

How often do we do girls' night? *Nearly never.*

Besides, this isn't a random celebration I can push off for another day. I'm here on serious business---girl code business. It doesn't get more serious than this.

"Earth to Evie... this is the second time you've zoned out. What's up?" Zelda, my best friend, snaps her fingers to grab my attention. I flinch and reach for my drink, hoping she won't notice my anxiety. Three days ago, her worthless, gold-digging fiancé dumped her five days shy of their wedding.

Tomorrow would have been the big day. It looms heavy like a dark cloud we need to wash away with booze and shit-talking gossip. We're not here to discuss my icky premonitions. We're here to mourn his existence and celebrate the divorce she surely avoided.

Good riddance, at least one of us dodged a bullet.

Zelda has a big heart and comes from good people who raised her to believe in true love. Her father would move the sun, moon and stars for his little girls' happiness and deep down the Haverty sisters expect the men in their life to do the same.

I don't have Arthur Haverty for a father. I have Evander Walsh. He doesn't see me as his little girl. I'm his prized possession, his greatest commodity to trade to the highest bidder. He's forgotten we came from nothing. Or maybe he just refuses to go back.

I reach for my drink and clink Zelda's glass. "Cheers. Don't mind me. My phone keeps buzzing." I make a show of pulling it out of my purse to check to see who's calling. I already know it's my father and I already know what he wants. He promised I had more time in Boston. Both my parents swore it would never come to this and I... I knew better than to trust them.

This reprieve was nothing more than temporary.

When the clock strikes 5:00, the bustling crowd at *Monty's Bar* thickens with college professors and stockbrokers filing in from High Street. There are too many people to keep track of the faces. Everyone looks suspicious. I lean my cheek into my shoulder and pretend to scratch my face. One quick scan confirms my suspicions. My father's goons are back on my tail.

I spot one loitering by a group of frat boys trolling for bootie. He looks out of place. They always look out of place. If I wasn't so annoyed by his presence, I'd give him extra points for trying to look like the average college student. That can't be easy for a man his age. I can tell he's dying to brush his hair. He keeps running his fingers through his course yellow strands, almost willing them back in place.

Zelda hops off her barstool and darts off to the ladies' room. As soon as she's gone, I place a napkin over her drink to shield it from any possible contamination and continue skimming the landscape. I know there is more than one. I can feel them closing in.

"You look spooked. What's up?" Zara, Zelda's bossy big sister, spots my anxious expression and demands an explanation. "You've been acting strange all night."

I lift my phone and show her my screen. "Don't tell Zelda anything. I don't want her to worry about me." I lead her gaze to a large, dark-haired man standing by the door. He doesn't bother hiding behind casual attire. He's a regular, and he knows I know who he is.

Zara jumps off her stool and swipes the phone from my

hand. "If your Dad knows where you are, why does he keep calling?"

I shrug and fake a chuckle. "The same reason he let me start graduate school knowing he'd never let me finish. He wants to feed me a lie. He wants to get his way without looking like the bad guy. Someone else is forcing his hand. No one tells the truth. Not my Mom. Not my Aunt Lily. Certainly not my father." I hear Zelda's clicking stilettos and lift my finger over my lips. "Don't say a word to her. She's got enough on her mind."

"You would not believe the fine slice of man I just crashed into on my way to the bathroom. Sweet Jesus, he smelled divine." Dazed with lust, Zelda climbs onto her stool in the most feminine manner possible then spends minutes fidgeting with her skirt. She subtly points out the gorgeous silver fox sitting two tables away as the man who's gotten her in such a tizzy.

"That's Carlo Novello." Zara bursts her sister's bubble by informing us he's one of Boston's biggest philanderers. I shake my head in disapproval, but Zelda doesn't seem as put off as she should. I can't blame her for seeking a distraction. Tomorrow's significance can't be easy. I only hope she knows what she's doing.

While Zara argues the merits of older, experienced men and Zelda lies, assuring her she's not interested, I hear the familiar sound of my Aunt Lily's voice. I look behind me, confused. No one's there. I'm losing my mind.

"Over here, Evie." Her raspy shrill finally breaks through the boisterous chatter and I spot her on the opposite side of the bar. She's in disguise. A wig of black curls hides her short auburn bob, and she's replaced her designer threads for clothes from my closet. She wastes no time and rushes to my side.

"What are you doing here?" I whisper and cringe at the sight. I'm not sure why she's come, but I can't believe my thirty-eight-year-old aunt fits into my jeans.

She hooks her arm into mine and leads me towards the restrooms. Her stiff posture makes me panic. I don't trust her. She's proven herself untrustworthy in the past. We pass the door marked *Ladies* and keep moving into the kitchen. I fear the worst and wiggle to break free. "Where are you taking me?"

"Hush up! You have little time. Your father is here, Evelyn. He's come to take you home." An unassuming man in the kitchen waves us through a side exit, and she thanks him for his help. I don't recognize him, but he appears to know Aunt Lily well.

"You need to run, Evie. Turn off your phone. Take I-90 West to New York and follow the signs. I left a map in the car. Use the money and ID to get lost in the city. We'll find you when the dust settles. If they drag you back to Hampstead, it'll be too late." She leads me towards a car I don't recognize parked in a nearby lot, then hands me the keys and an envelope full of cash.

I'm utterly stunned. A thousand questions stream through my head, but only one tumbles loose from my lips. "Who are we?"

"I can't explain, sweetheart. I should have helped you sooner. But I didn't know your father would really go through with it. I packed your bags and threw them into the trunk." She throws her arms around my neck and pushes me into the driver's seat.

"Oh, no, I can't leave. What about school?" I fight back tears of grief and tremble with panic. New York? Alone? No one ever lets me go anywhere alone. What will I do there alone?

"Please, go! Now! They'll know you're missing." She shoves me harder, and I start the ignition. "I love you, Evie. We'll find you and make sure you're okay. But you need to disappear." She taps the door to say goodbye and I speed off into the night.

As I turn into traffic, heavy tears obscure oncoming headlights and I wipe my face clean with my sleeve. I check my rearview mirror. No one's following. Not yet. They must know I'm gone by now. I hit the signal to enter the highway, glance over my shoulder, and hit the gas.

How can they force me to marry Sterling Gallagher? He hurts people. He hurts women. They know he won't spare me.

Lily's right, I need to disappear. My father won't give up easily. It's not in his nature. That's why he's so successful.

And that's what hurts most. He has enough money and power. He gains nothing but favor—-closer ties to the almighty Gallagher family.

Through me, he'll finally be one of them.

Is that really all I'm worth?

EVE

"Are you ready, dear?" Aunt Lillian rests her palms on my shoulders as I stare motionless into the smudged vanity mirror. A weak smile touches her lips but quickly fades. I know she feels guilty for bringing me home, but you don't say no to my father.

Not with so much on the line.

I nod and hand her the string of heirloom pearls I plan to wear. "Almost. Are the cars here?"

She nods once and fastens my necklace, brushing my hair down with her fingers. "Your parents said they'll wait downstairs. They've asked Mary Alice to pack two bags and I'll take the rest tomorrow."

My heart leaps into my throat. "My things? Why am I taking things? The wedding isn't for three more days."

"Hugh Gallagher thinks it's best if you live with them until the wedding. They fear you'll run away again." She turns to shield her tears but the sound of honking horns makes her return to my side. "They're waiting. I know it's hard, but please, don't give them reasons to make it harder on you."

I panic, terrified to leave the safety of my bedroom. "I can't run in this dress."

"One step at a time, Evie. You'll be okay. Good things happen every day. Don't lose faith." She gives me a kiss on the cheek and helps me gather my things.

Faith? I don't know what that means anymore. I don't have time for faith. I don't have time for anything anymore.

If I'd known I'd have so few happy years, I would have done things differently. I would have traveled or dated. That's a joke. No one lets me do anything. Besides school, what have I really done?

This feels so unfair. I thought I'd marry a kind man who loves me. I took it for granted. In my mind, an older, mild-mannered gentleman with dark hair, dazzling blue eyes, and the cutest dimples when he smiles would sweep me off my feet and promise to love me forever.

Why does my mind always return to him? He's nothing to me. Those silly dreams do me no good.

I wish I'd never had them.

In three days, I become Mrs. Sterling Gallagher. The moment I recite those vows, my heart will die and every dream I've ever had will crumble to dust.

I can't believe my life is over.

TWO

DEACON

"Which one, sir? The blue or the red?" My assistant holds a pair of silk ties and repeats his question. He knows I'm ignoring him. It's such a mundane detail on a day like today. I lift my wrist and fasten my cuff link, gnashing my teeth at the sight of the tiny *G* engraved in platinum. These were my father's favorite cuff links. It's fitting he should be here in some capacity since he's responsible for it all.

I turn to Samuel, acknowledging his effort, then return to my place at the window. "I'll wear one of the black ones. Just pick whichever one you like. They're almost all the same." I wave him away, hoping he takes his time retrieving it from my closet. I want to be alone with my thoughts.

He groans and wags his head with dismay. "Mr. Gallagher, please don't make my job difficult. Mrs. Baxter begged me not to dress you entirely in black."

"You don't dress me. Tell my sister..." I lose my train of thought and cut my words mid-sentence. My gaze drifts to a tiny caravan of cars arriving through the steel gates. It must be them. Everyone else is here.

"Tell me what?" Rory, my kid sister, stomps into the room and snatches the gaudy ties from Sam's hands. "Enough black. You look like a mortician. This is an important day for our family. All the Gallaghers and all the old families are here. They look to you for leadership, Deacon. You need to set a good example and stop brooding."

She snaps her head in Sam's direction. "Get my brother a nice, crisp white dress shirt on the double and he'll wear the blue tie. It goes with his eyes." She tosses the tie in my face and sends Sam on his way.

I nudge past her and throw the tie on the floor. "Woman, you are six years younger than me. Do not tell me what to do." Ever since our mother passed away, she's under the impression she's the new matriarch of the family. She's thirty-five and acts sixty. "This is not a good day. I'm sick to my stomach and I've taken too many antacids. No one cares what I wear. They all want to see Sterling's bride." I catch my words and clench my fists, furious for calling her that. I should have never let it come to this.

What kind of man am I?

Furious with my myself and eager to catch a glimpse of her face, I step away and return to the window. Three cars park side by side and the usual suspects file out dressed in their glittering best.

Such horrible people—*but who am I to cast stones?*

Evander Walsh's smug face beams with pride while his complicit wife fidgets with the seam on her dress. They hold hands and make a beeline to the front door, delighted to throw their daughter to the wolves.

The second car carries Daniel Kennedy, their family attorney and the most ruthless shark that ever infested legal waters. He's here to finalize last-minute details and ensure Evander gets everything he wants. He doesn't represent

Evie. No one represents her. Last I heard, he's haggled Sterling's prenuptial agreement to the bare bones.

Serves him right. You don't marry a woman like Eve Walsh for financial gain.

At last, Eve makes her appearance.

Two bodyguards stream out first. They hold the door and surround a slight figure dressed in red. She doesn't move as fast as the others, and her companions don't rush her. Her palpable sorrow makes my galloping heart ache with remorse. How on earth will I survive the evening?

"How far did she get?" Rory looks over my shoulder and hooks the tie over my head. She moves so quickly, I hardly feel her shrug the new shirt on my arms.

"She made it to Manhattan. Can you believe that? She had a nice day at The Plaza Hotel and saw a few exhibits at the Met. Her father's people caught up with her the next day and dragged her back to Boston. They made Lilian bring her here." I keep talking while I watch Eve walk the cobbled pathway towards the door. When she reaches the steps leading into the garden, a sympathetic bodyguard offers his arm. She hesitates, ducking her head timidly before she takes it.

The unnatural sight infuriates me but its a sight I'll have to see for the rest of my life. Unless I stop this.

I am my father's son. Everyone expects me to turn into him. So why do I have to prove them wrong?

I run my fingers through my hair and look down at my chest. "Why am I wearing a white shirt?"

"It makes you look five years younger, Deacon. Stop trying to be an old man. And stop punishing yourself. You did everything you could, right?" She hands me my father's cufflinks and averts her gaze, unable to hide her disappointment.

Samuel returns in an agitated state. His pale face looks red from choked anger. "Your guests have gathered, sir. I fear your nephew is already making a terrible impression on his intended." He wipes his brow with a handkerchief and waits for instructions.

"I'm on my way. We might as well get right to it." I straighten my tie and turn to face the window.

"She's not out there anymore, Deacon. She's downstairs mingling with a man you don't trust alone with your dogs because he's mean to animals." Her soft voice breaks as she brings her misty eyes to mine.

"Dad did this, not you. Cut Sterling off and Evander won't find him so desirable. If you disown him, Walsh won't make her go through with it. Why shouldn't you? Because the great Deacon Gallagher won't go against his own family? You won't go against Hugh, the brother who hates you?" She sighs and presses her hand into the doorframe to hold herself steady.

She makes it sound so easy, as if it's something I haven't considered. Like I'm not dying to call off this ridiculous farce and save Eve from a misery I don't want to imagine.

I've watched Evelyn Walsh for years. She caught my eye when I had no business looking and no matter how hard I try, I can't purge her from my thoughts.

For three years, ever since I crowned her Hampstead High School's 100th Annual Homecoming Queen, I've wanted her more than air. The memory lingers sweetly on my mind like a fragrant perfume I can't shake free from my senses.

Her smile captured my heart. Her long honey-brown hair and bright green eyes made my pulse race with adrenaline. The black and white sash with the words Homecoming Queen draped awkwardly over the full bust of her pink sequined dress made me harder than a slab of tungsten steel. She looked exquisite. None of my photos will ever do her justice.

As appalling as that sounds, I know for a fact she was four days past her eighteenth birthday when I first took notice. It's small consolation when you're a thirty-eight-year-old man getting hot and bothered over someone in high school but I assure you, this isn't who I am.

I'm a successful businessman, a pillar of my community, and the patriarch of my family. I wouldn't condone this behavior in others and I can't allow it in myself.

Evelyn Walsh is the greatest weakness I've ever known, and I can't risk ushering that kind of vulnerability into my life. I would never recover. But that doesn't mean my heart isn't torn in two.

Until four months ago, Sterling had no intention to see this engagement through. He's known Eve since they were children and shown no interest beyond tormenting her. When he made his decision, I said no. I wanted to choke the life from his vicious body or at the very least disown him for broaching the subject.

Shame prevented me from tearing him to shreds. Eve's half my age. Did I hope to win her for myself? I've known her parents all her life. Surely, she thinks of me as an old man.

My brother, Hugh, pleaded his son's case, and he's a fool if he thinks I don't understand his motives. He wants this more than his son, and he's using Sterling the same way Evander is using Eve.

"Ready?" Rory walks into the hallway and adjusts her heavy diamond necklace.

"Let's get this over with." I nod and close the door to my study. The sooner we begin the sooner I can crawl back into my room and drown my sorrows in a bottle of whisky.

We walk in silence, waiting for someone to say something that might make a difference. She knows we tried. With Lilian's help, we tried to give Eve a head start and help her vanish long enough to make Evander come to his senses.

Can I do more? I can't go against my siblings the way my father did. He ruled everyone with an iron fist. He ruled through sheer terror. I promised myself I'd do better.

But I am curious about one thing.

When we get to the end of the hall, I hold out my hand to keep the footman from opening the door to the ballroom.

"I know why this marriage upsets me. Why does it upset you?"

She takes a deep breath but keeps her gaze fixed to the door. "Evie's a beautiful soul. And we all know Sterling destroys beautiful things. It just breaks my heart imagining what he'll do to her."

THREE

EVE

There are eighteen steps between me and the ballroom. If I take five seconds to climb each one, that gives me another minute and a half of freedom. It could take years to find a way out of this hell. But right now, this time is mine and mine alone.

Trembling with panic, I place a shaky foot on the staircase, and feel it slip on the polished marble. With seventeen more to go, I may never make it in these shoes. My gaze falls to the hem of my dress and I gather the billowy fabric to keep from falling. Two more steps and my hummingbird heart wants to fly out of my chest. But I press on with a fourth, fifth and sixth step until my wobbly knees make me stop.

With each labored breath, my half-naked chest heaves into my line of vision. How will I ever live down this humiliation? My breasts will be the first thing anyone sees. I stall on the eighth step and curse my mother's trashy taste.

I wanted a simple black dress, but she wouldn't hear of it. She insisted on this ridiculous red rag because she claims it compliments my figure. It's vulgar and garish, with hardly enough silk to hide my nipples.

"Evelyn, walk faster. Everyone's waiting on you." *Speak of the devil, and the devil appears.* My mother finally stops socializing long enough to check on me. Her hand presses into my back and I recoil at her touch. I'm furious and the more she pretends everything is peachy, the more I simmer with rage.

This is her dream come true. She has wealth, jewels, and a grand home full of servants, but my father's new money can't buy respect. Both my parents hope my marriage will bring them esteem and favors for years to come. In six days, they become Gallaghers by default. God answered their prayers. They bartered their only daughter in exchange for respectability and have no room for remorse.

I'll play along for now. I've lived my entire life in my father's gilded cage. Sterling's won't be any different. If I need to pretend to be a dutiful wife to throw everyone off my scent, then so be it. One day, someone will let their guard down. And when they do, I'll be gone.

Five more steps and five more to go.

"Stop pushing me. I'm not used to walking in heels this high. You'll make me fall." My voice grates through clenched teeth as I choke back the pain in my breaking heart. There's no way she can mistake my fury. She's known me since birth. Outraged by her tone-deaf intrusion on my last seconds of freedom, I charge ahead in search of escape, but my last step brings me to a crashing stop.

I've entered another world, and no description will do it justice. It's so breathtaking I almost forget it's nothing more than a beautiful prison.

My presence draws immediate stares. The checkerboard marble floor echoes against my heels and peels people away from their drinks and frivolous conversations. Someone sneers with derision. Most look on with pity, but a few others turn their nose in restrained displeasure.

I'm not one of them and I never will be.

With nowhere to go, I tread forward and use my hand to cover my plunging neckline. No one else is dressed this provocatively. I'm out of my league and it shows. All around me, sumptuous flowers, gorgeous gowns, jewels that make my dainty pearls look like childish trinkets, shine brighter than the crystal chandeliers dazzling overhead.

Sterling spots me from across the room. Although our eyes meet, he makes no move towards me. I'm glad of it. The longer he keeps his distance, the happier I'll be. After today, everything will change, and moments of peace will be few and far between.

I take a flute of champagne from a passing tray and guzzle the contents. When another tray buzzes by, I grab a second and nurse it while I pretend to mingle. As much I want to float away on the wings of inebriation, I'm better off keeping my wits. If I don't look out for myself, no one will.

Fortunately, the crowd's fixation with me quickly dies and I creep unnoticed to the back of the room. No one cares about the *Walsh girl*, and they care even less about Sterling. No one came here for us. They're here to pay fealty to their god.

As 7:00 approaches, the whispering herd of sycophants move like a school of fish and gather by the foot of yet another staircase. They clap, clink their glasses with over-sized baubles and stare in adoration at the elegant man making his descent.

It's Deacon. Of course, it's him. Everyone in Hampstead waits on pins and needles for the tiniest glimpse of Deacon Gallagher.

Not long ago, I felt the same way.

Not anymore.

FOUR

DEACON

W E ALL MAKE MISTAKES, THEY'RE AN INEVITABLE PART of life. Sometimes clarity is swift. We have a visceral reaction to whatever action we take, and we make immediate amends. You need to trust your gut instincts but I fear I surrendered mine long ago.

A week after my twenty-sixth birthday, my father left me the keys to his kingdom. He made me an absolute ruler over my family, friends and everyone living in the small town my family built---our feudal land, Hampstead, Massachusetts.

Was I prepared? No, not by a long shot. It made no difference to him. I was his firstborn and whether I liked it or not, I had to rise to the challenge.

Despite my inexperience, he castrated his board of directors and left me controlling interest of his multi-billion-dollar corporation. He made me wealthier beyond my wildest dreams and left my siblings nothing but subservient to my will.

The cruel stipulations of his will placed me in charge of my family's welfare, but powerful enough to seize everything I grant them on a moment's notice. That's the way the old man wanted it.

His father and his father's father did the same. It's how we Gallaghers keep power concentrated at the top.

I promised myself I would never be like my father, and I've spent the last fifteen years ignoring my instincts to be as ruthless as him.

No one needs this much power. It's an arrangement that breeds bitterness and mistrust. It keeps the rest of my family at arms' length and a man in my position needs his family. Especially since every year it becomes less likely I'll have one of my own.

Through my initial patronage, my sister amassed her own fortune and made herself financially independent from the family. I hoped our brother would do the same, but he can't move past his bitterness. Nothing placates him. If I gave him half of what I have, he'd burn through it in a week and demand more. He wants what I have.

Nothing less will do.

In typical fashion, Hugh sought an easy fix at someone else's expense. And I was right to shut him down. I went with my gut and I gave him an unequivocal *no*. But he wouldn't let it go.

He prodded for weeks. He used guilt and accused me of being a bully, just like our father. It was a mistake to give in. I'm certain I felt it seconds after I agreed, but ignored my better sense. I allowed myself to be manipulated because I hate being compared to my father.

And now I can't understand why. Dad took whatever he wanted.

If he could see what I see, the most beautiful girl in the world standing alone in the back of the room with tears in her eyes, he'd send everyone home. He'd call off the wedding and take her for himself.

No explanations. No remorse. He'd make sure Evelyn Walsh never looked so sad again.

For the first time in my life, I wish I was *exactly* like my father.

The moment my feet step onto the checkerboard floor, I shove my way through the dense crowd of silk gowns, tiaras and tuxedos, and head straight to her place by the back wall. As I tear through unfamiliar townspeople, I should really know by name, my gaze never strays far from that red dress. What kind of material is that? I swear it defies gravity. It doesn't matter, I'll buy her a hundred more just like it.

What am I saying? This is Sterling's engagement party, not mine.

The more I struggle to make my way, the more people cross my path. I weave through mothers introducing unmarried daughters and family heaping undeserved praise for Sterling. Hugh barges forth and demands I introduce him as a host. I can't deal with him. Instead of answering, I place my hands on his shoulders and move him aside. He's the reason this is happening and the last person I want to see.

I can't think, I can't see straight, I just need to get to her.

At long last, I reach the end of the room, and she's gone. I look from side to side and scan the ballroom for signs of red. She's disappeared. It doesn't make any sense. She was just here.

Panic settles into my bones and my heart stings with despair. Did she sneak away? On my way to question a server, I spy movement coming from the East Hall. A quick flash of red darts into my office and my heart soars.

Treading lightly, I slink into the hall and peek through a

crack in the door. Sweat dampens my forehead. My stomach churns so loudly, I'm certain she'll discover me lurking. When my eyes adjust to the dark, I see a faint figure emerge from the shadows.

It's too dark to see her face, but the sound of rustling silk confirms my suspicions. While her back faces the door, I creep into the room and wait in the darkness. I long to step closer, but fear I'll send her running.

"And why are you smiling? There's nothing to smile about today." Her whisper catches me off guard. She's not looking at me. *Can she see me?*

"Who keeps a painting like this in his own house? Such a conceited man. I'll bet you're used to women throwing themselves at you night and day." She giggles and I lean into the light to glimpse her face. She's talking to herself. No, she's talking to my painting.

Good god, I hate that painting. My mother had it commissioned for my thirty-fifth birthday. It's ridiculous. She wanted me to hang it over the fireplace, but it's so over the top, I keep it hidden in here.

She must think I enjoy staring at myself all day.

"Why me? Why didn't you make him choose someone else? There are so many girls who'd love to be his wife." She sighs as she rests her elbows on my desk. I can hardly breathe. She's so lovely, so innocent, there's no doubt this is far beyond what Sterling deserves.

Why have I allowed this?

My lovesick gaze feasts on every little inch of her flawless face. My hands itch to touch her. I feel like such a coward. When she stands, I watch her prowl closer to the painting, and smirk at my vulgar display of vanity.

I'm dying to apologize and desperate to declare my intentions. *What intentions?* I'll sound like a lunatic.

She's not meant for me.

"Did *you* pick me personally, Deacon? Did *you* choose me to be your nephew's wife?" Her sweet, seductive whisper transforms into a brittle grouse and with a petulant huff, she turns her back on the wall.

My skin prickles with Déjà vu. It's fleeting but profound enough to pull the air from my lungs and make me leap from the shadows.

"No, I didn't choose you. But it wasn't up to me." Moved by madness, my chaotic words tumble out before I've considered how she'll respond.

She gasps, jumps back and almost falls on the hem of her dress. "Mr. Gallagher! I'm sorry, I shouldn't be here."

I close the distance between us and watch her green eyes grow wide with fear. Her cheeks flush pink and her breasts rise as she takes a shaky breath. She's stunning, a work of art too beautiful to drink in all at once.

Do I care that she's too young for me? Everything about Evie Walsh exudes youthful innocence and untainted mouthwatering virtue. Does that make me a cad? She's my nephew's age, but I don't have children of my own. We'd make our own family.

Lost in a daze of desire, my eyes rake over her, undressing her from head to toe while she stands and waits for me give her room. There are so many things I want to say, but I can hardly remember to breathe, let alone find words to speak.

"I should go." She lifts her hands to hold me at bay while she creeps back, cornered against the wall and trapped like a wild animal.

Suddenly aware of my overzealous posture, I step back and give her space to feel safe. "Don't go. You asked if I wanted you for my nephew and the answer is *no*. I don't want this."

I draw one step closer and the scent of her perfumed skin awakens my foggy senses. My mind spins with feverish lust. I'm dying to touch her, pull her quivering limbs close and drown in her taste, but propriety prevents it. What an unfamiliar emotion—strength in weakness. I thought love would make me fall apart. Evie makes me feel like I could scale a mountain just to fall at her feet.

Her tense shoulders fall to her side and her sad expression returns. "I don't believe you. You're Deacon Gallagher. Nothing happens in Hampstead without your approval."

She weaves past my intrusive presence but I catch her hand in mine and spin us towards the wall. Her eyes widen with shock. Her pouty lips part so perfectly, I take it as an invitation to devour them. I've lost my mind. It's more than that. Madness visits me like never before. My tongue sweeps in and muffles her brief protest. Thank goodness its over as soon as it begins. My darling girl throws her arms around my neck and melts into my arms.

"You don't have to do this, Eve. Tell them no." I run my finger down the line of her jaw and ask her to take the first step. If she tells her parents no, I'll back her up. I'll take care of her. We can be together.

She shakes her head once and her sad expression returns. "I thought you understood. It's too late."

"Evelyn!" A woman's voice calls from the hall and Evie startles with fear. She rushes to the door as footsteps draw near. "Evelyn!"

"I need to go. That's my mother. I'm sorry, Deacon."

Sorry?

FIVE

EVE

"There she is!" The safety and silence of Deacon's office explode with the shrill sound of my mother's voice. She approaches with Sterling by her side, and I can tell by the look in her eyes, she's part relieved and part furious. I don't know how long I've been missing, but she feared the worst.

She fears her version of the worst. She fears I might escape and ruin her plans. If she only knew I've spent the last five minutes exploring Deacon Gallagher's mouth with my tongue, she'd revise her version of the worst likely scenario.

I amble near the wall and take my time to reach them. Hugh Gallagher, Sterling's father, walks nearby, sipping a glass of champagne and looking strangely ill at ease. He quirks a brow and looks past me, perhaps trying to determine where I've been. If he suspects anything, he says nothing.

Ever since I arrived in Hampstead, I've been on autopilot. I go through everyday motions and try to pretend I'm someone else, living a happier life somewhere far away. It isn't so bad. Just when you think you'll die of a broken heart, numbness sets in and defiance pushes you forward.

It was a mistake to kiss him. It was a mistake to taste something I can't have. Hope is dangerous. I lowered my defenses for the chance to hear his voice, but I never expected him to kiss me.

It doesn't matter. What's done is done. For years, I've held onto the crazy fantasy that Deacon Gallagher never married because he and I were meant for one another. I'm a foolish girl with dreams too big for my cage.

For obvious reasons, I've never shared my feelings with anyone. Not even Zelda. It's too embarrassing to confess something so immature. The truth would have blown her mind.

Like an adolescent schoolgirl, I held out and shunned boys who couldn't hold a candle to the only man I've ever loved. Deep down, I felt certain our paths would cross again, and when they did, we'd fall madly in love and live happily ever after.

That isn't what happened. We kissed. He wanted to clear his conscience, and I let myself fall prey to his charm.

His answer was no. For a moment, relief washed over me. He didn't choose me for Sterling and didn't plan my ruin. But he won't do anything to stop it. He expects me to go against the power of Evander Walsh.

How do I tell him I have the financial resources of a toddler? My father's goons took the only money I had when they cornered me in New York. When I tried to call the police, my parents threatened me with homelessness. And I have little doubt they'd pull that trigger.

How do I confess to Deacon Gallagher that I'm a grown woman without a cent to my name? My father kept me from making my own money and paid my bills through my aunt. I've got nothing but coins in a *Hello Kitty* wallet I've owned since I was fifteen years old. No checking or savings accounts and no credit cards in my name. They knew what they were doing, making me completely dependent, and I was an idiot to trust them.

I won't live off my friends. With my father's connections, I may not land a decent job. And if I can't work, I'll wind up being a burden on someone else. Believe me, I've thought this through, and I can't find a way out.

I don't expect his help. His loyalty lies with his family. But I need to keep my distance and stop wishing for more. One more second in his arms and the shattered pieces of my broken heart will disintegrate into dust.

Sterling steps away from my mother and offers his hand in an uncommonly kind manner. My eyes flash to his, but instead of making his typical rude remark, he tilts his head and makes a motion towards the dance floor.

"Join me for a dance. We should talk." He offers a fake smile, but instead of questioning his motives, I give him the benefit of the doubt. What choice do I have?

"Were you looking for a way out?" His cruel remark seems fitting. I'm glad it doesn't take much for the real Sterling to appear. He chuckles under his breath and I lift my gaze to his. He can't hurt me. I have little heart left to break.

I shake my head demurely and sigh. There's no sense baiting him. I don't have the strength to put up a fight. "I was searching for the ladies' room."

He nods and wraps his arm around my shoulders in a possessive gesture. My skin crawls, but I take a deep breath and remember the bigger picture. No one will save me but me. If he thinks I want to run, he'll keep a closer watch. It's best to make him think I've resigned myself to the inevitable.

My tactic works, and his expression softens. "You shouldn't show so much skin, Evie. I don't like men staring at you."

"My mother insisted on this dress. You know this isn't my style. I've been uncomfortable all night." I spot Deacon approaching and I pout coquettishly.

What am I doing? This is beneath me. I can't flirt with Sterling---*he's repugnant.*

When we reach the dance floor, he spins me once and slams me into his chest. It's all for show. He wants to appear gallant in front of my father and the Gallagher clan. As soon as we receive the requisite applause, he mumbles through his smile, like a ventriloquist. "We need to talk about the prenup, Evie. Your Dad is trying to screw me."

I stare, confused, then bat my lashes, like the concept of money is far beyond my grasp. He knows nothing about me. I'm certain he's unaware I have a business degree. "Is there a question in there?"

He leans in and smells my perfume. "You smell nice. Yes, there's a question. Tell him to call off his lawyer. I'm sorry, that's not a question, but you know what I mean. My father plans to take half of whatever I get out of this marriage, and your father wants to make me work for him. I'm doing all the work and getting the short end of the stick." A deep scowl appears, then disappears when my parents waltz by. I didn't expect this level of honesty.

"Are you kids having fun?" My father's exaggerated laugh makes me turn away, but Sterling matches it with his own boisterous cackle. They're a perfect match for one another, both self-centered bullies trying to disguise their mutual animosity. Sterling's cutthroat personality is precisely what my father wanted from me.

Unfortunately, he doesn't have Walsh blood and my father doesn't trust him to stick around. That prenuptial agreement makes Sterling as much of a prisoner as me.

Annoyed with their tit for tat, I look over his shoulder and search the floor for Deacon. He's easy to spot, smiling from ear to ear as he makes the rounds and greets his guests. He's not the least bit concerned with me.

And why would he be? Women from every corner of the room flock to him like he's the second coming of Jesus and they're lepers looking for a cure. His flirtatious banter makes them giggle, shielding their expensive veneers as they snort like rabid hyenas on the prowl for the ultimate prize.

My jealous heart rises from its own death and rips in two. My knees buckle, my head spins and I fall forward into Sterling's arms. I'm shocked when he's decent enough to catch me.

"You're making a spectacle, Evelyn. Maybe you two should take a seat." My parents' impeccable timing never ceases to amaze me.

Still fresh from haggling with Hugh Gallagher's attorney, my father asserts his dominance by cutting in and steering me out of Sterling's embrace. His audacity and condescending tone instantly transform Sterling's mood. He'll kiss Deacon's ass, but he's not about to let his *ne'er-do-well* nephew seize the upper hand.

Sterling sneers defiantly, catches my arm and snatches me out of my father's grasp. I topple against my father, then catch myself on Sterling's chest. They lunge forward with clenched fists and grunt like gorillas.

"We're adults. We'll decide when we sit or when we dance." Sterling pulls me into his body, then closes his bicep around my neck. He holds me so tightly, he can't see he's cut off my air. He can't see he's dangling me off the ground.

While they spew insults and scream about money, my father attempts to pull me away. But not to save me. *God, no.* The man doesn't have a paternal bone in his body.

He doesn't notice I'm gasping for air. He wants to reclaim his leverage.

Desperate for help, I flail my arms to get my mother's attention, but she accuses me of being dramatic. It's the same song and dance since I was little.

Don't make a fuss, Evie, and for God's sake don't embarrass us.

The argument intensifies and draws attention from the crowd. The more Sterling rages, the tighter he clenches. There's no room to wiggle and no air to cry for help. Seconds turn to minutes and the world blurs. Lights grow dim and voices fade to muffled whispers.

This was not the way I wanted to die. *Not here.* Not in this horrible dress. I didn't want to spend my last moments sandwiched between the two men I despise the most, while they argue about contracts and who has the greater right to mistreat me.

As the room goes dark, I'm filled with one solitary regret. I wish I could have shared one night with Deacon. One night to last me a lifetime. Even if it meant nothing to him. Even if that's all he could give. If I could pretend for one night that he was mine and I was his, I could endure anything.

Even this.

SIX

DEACON

"Wonderful party, Deacon." Someone shouts an empty compliment, but I'm too frazzled to look up.

"Another great one, Gallagher!" I wave into the air and fake a smile, lost in my tiny world of unimaginable anguish. Evie's disappointed expression haunts me every step of the way.

Do I love her? I hardly know her. Can you love a woman you spent so little time with? I don't know. But she moves me. She moves me more than any woman I've ever known. And when she pulled out of my arms, I felt a hole in my chest where my heart used to be.

"They make a lovely couple. You must be so proud." My cousin Gina's innocent comment knocks the wind clear out of my lungs. I skid on the polished floor and nearly miss a passing server. My eye twitches with fury. Rage engulfs my senses. If she wasn't a woman and geriatric, I'd knock her on her ass.

"Thank you, Gina. Please, have something to drink." I nudge a server between us and fly away, ramming straight into a gaggle of Canada Geese, overgrown debutantes hell bent on dragging me down the aisle before they pass their most fertile years.

Sorry ladies, look somewhere else.

"Deacon, darling. Where on earth are you going?" Celia Humphries, one of my most relentless admirers, hooks her arm in mine and leads me into an impromptu meeting with the Hampstead Ladies' Auxiliary Club. There's no escape. The horde surrounds me, regaling me all at once with mindless chatter that sends me into a tailspin of nods, handshakes and cliché statements about the weather.

From the corner of my eye, I spot Sterling and Eve, dancing cheek to cheek under the brilliant lights of the chandeliers. My wretched soul sinks into a pool of despair. Has she come to accept him? No, I don't believe her heart could turn so swiftly. I need to believe she's taken the path of least resistance.

What choice have I given her? We kissed. Did I make any declaration? No, I gave her nothing but lust.

Bitter truth strikes me like a kick to the groin. I'm going about this all wrong. These aren't my instincts. I've buried those for so long, I've almost forgotten what they feel like.

Her father trapped her in an impossible position. He's a ruthless man. His reputation precedes him. If he wants her to marry Sterling, then he's left nothing to chance. She's not complying out of love and devotion. She's got no other option.

Unless I'm her option. Is that what she wants? Does she want me to...no, I don't need to finish that sentence----it ends there. *Does she want me?*

I'm forty-one years old. *That's not so ancient.* A twenty-year age difference isn't insurmountable. I take care of myself. Women find me attractive. It can't all be about the money. *Can it?*

I stop to re-examine my features until I conclude I must be aesthetically pleasing. This is no time for self-doubt. And it's not all about looks. From an evolutionary standpoint, I'm a sound choice. If she wants a large family, I have the means to take care of our children. She could do so much worse. And she will, if she goes through with this wedding.

More women gather, threading me into their web and blinding me with jewels meant more for a coronation, not a simple engagement party. I keep my eyes trained on Evie's honey-brown hair, floating aimlessly through a sea of snobs with nothing but contempt in their hearts for the loveliest girl in the room. Her parents might be the worst offenders.

I spot them near the couple, surely chastising their daughter for some new grievance they've manufactured from air. She shrinks into Sterling, and he wraps his arms around her, stabbing the knife deeper the tighter he holds her.

There's no sense in looking away. *I need to see this.* If I don't act, I'll stare at this heart-wrenching view for the rest of my miserable life.

My obsession draws me closer. Like a moth to a flame, I drift through the swarm of whirling bodies waltzing around the tiny spectacle at the center of the dance floor. It's not about Eve. The men appear focused on one another. I've seen this a million times.

It's the prelude to fists, and they've placed her in an awkward position. She's stuck between two bickering men with no end in sight.

From a different angle, I watch her arms reach out for help. She's frightened, and when she turns to her mother, the woman instantly dismisses her concerns. It's no surprise. I've known Holly Walsh since high school, and she couldn't nurture a plant, much less a human being.

I don't know how Eve turned out so sweet.

Wait a minute, something's wrong. My heart races as I step closer and finally examine Eve's expression. He's not holding her in a passionate embrace. He's so focused on Evander Walsh he doesn't feel he's strangling the life out of Eve.

Propriety flees and panic reigns. My feet move before my brain processes the information. He's cut off her air. Who knows how long she's fought for breath---how could I be so stupid? As adrenaline and rage surges through my veins, I fly through the herd, square my shoulders, swing my arm and punch Sterling right in the jaw.

It's the perfect hit and I'm so concerned with catching Eve, I hardly feel the impact. She takes a tiny gasp, not nearly enough to fill her lungs, then faints into my arms.

How many times will I fail her?

Every instinct I've suppressed returns with a vengeance. Enough is enough.

"Stop the music. Call the paramedics and everyone get the hell out of my house right now."

SEVEN

EVE

He saved me. I saw him coming. His blue eyes turned black, his angry lips yelled something I couldn't hear. When his fist flew into Sterling's face, my lungs filled with air. I felt him fold me gently into his embrace. The world fell silent and dark.

But I didn't die. He saved me. Deacon saved me.

Oh no, Deacon saved me.

This is a significant turn of events that I can't sweep under the rug. I had a near death experience. In my final moments, I had one regret involving the man I love.

This requires unavoidable action. It's a sign. There's no sense arguing over something as obvious as this.

A sign is a sign. And this is a sign.

Do you know what this means? I rub the sleep off my eyes and shake my fists at the ceiling. "I get it! I know what I need to do."

"Evie? Are you awake?" My mother barges into my room and storms towards my bed. Suddenly aware of my surroundings, my eyes scan from left to right. I look down, sideways and past her towards the door. *Where the hell am I?* Did they really bring me to Sterling's house after all?

Rory Baxter, Deacon's younger sister, darts through the threshold and chases her down. She kicks off her heels and sprints into action, determined to beat her before she reaches my end of the room.

"What's happening?" I tuck my arms into the bedsheet and use the blanket to shield myself from my mother's wrath. Thanks to Rory's long legs, I don't need to. She flings herself on the mattress and places her body between us, keeping my mother from coming too close.

"Holly, the doctor said no visitors and Deacon insists she be left alone to heal. Don't make me call security." Rory sits on the edge of the bed and stretches her arms like a fence. She looks over her shoulder and gives me a wink. I'm not sure what that means, but I'm happy she's here.

"The doctor didn't mean me, for heaven's sake. I'm her mother." She stomps her pump and tries an underhanded move that is swiftly thwarted.

"I came to bring her home. We'll call our doctor and I'm sure he'll clear her." My mother tries again to weave past her arms, but Rory stays firm. "We have to prepare for her wedding, Rory. It's the day after tomorrow!"

My fuzzy brain puts two and two together and harsh reality sets in. *The wedding is still on.* Sterling almost killed me and the wedding is still on.

Why would I assume my parents cancelled those plans after Sterling nearly strangled the life out of me? It makes more sense for them to move ahead as if nothing ever happened. There's too much at stake to hold anyone accountable.

I duck my head under the covers and laugh at my

perpetual optimism. *I'm still marrying Sterling.* This makes perfect sense. It would have been more outrageous if Evander and Holly Walsh suddenly chosen *not* to marry me off to the man who almost killed me.

What was I thinking?

"Holly, I specifically banned you from this room. Get out, now, or I'll have you arrested for trespassing." Deacon appears at the doorway and his booming voice fills the room.

I peek over the sheet and drink him in from head to toe. My weary heart comes to life. I've never seen him in blue jeans. How could he keep such a feast all to himself? And why does he wear everything so well? No man needs to flaunt this kind of beauty. *It's indulgent.* He's forty-one and still fills out every nook and cranny of a well-worn pair of blue jeans. The denim fabric molds beautifully to his thick muscular legs and leaves nothing to my lovesick imagination. I didn't know him in his twenties but if I did, I'm certain I would have thrown myself at his feet and begged him to make me his love slave. This is cruel.

Frustrated with my mother's defiance, he takes an exasperated breath and his massive chest heaves. I release a silent gasp when his thin cashmere sweater reveals every sculpted detail of his rippled torso. He's heavenly, more beautiful than my nastiest dreams. I clench my fists and wiggle my feet under the covers, desperate to feel him close.

"Eve looks much better now, Deacon. She's ready to come home. Aren't you, Eve?" My horrible mother cranes her neck and narrows her beady eyes to intimidate me into compliance. I can't leave. Not yet. Not until Deacon has his way with me.

I know I'm only prolonging the inevitable and my father won't let this insubordination go unpunished, but if this is Deacon's home, then an extra day is all I need.

I summon the strength to defy my mother, then swallow hard with angst. Fortunately, the tenderness in my throat brings back the memory of her indifference. She stood, watched, and did nothing to help me. Only Deacon came to my rescue. Maybe this is fate.

For dramatic effect, I lift my hand to my neck and whisper a faint reply. "No, I don't feel well enough to travel." My eyes shift to Deacon's, still waiting by the door. "Do I have to leave?"

He doesn't hesitate to answer. He flings the door open and points to my mother. "Holly. Out. Now. If Eve feels better tomorrow, we'll call you. No promises."

His stern commands make me squirm with excitement. And for a moment, my spirits lift. Will he take me up on my offer?

I shouldn't dare hope for more, but this could be what carries me through Saturday. One night with Deacon might make up for all the miserable nights with Sterling. It's the only hope I have.

But I should know better than to hope.

"I'm not leaving without my daughter!" In a bold, dramatic move, my mother hurls herself onto the bed and covers me with her body. With little thought to my condition, she lands so hard, she knocks the wind out of my lungs.

Rory screams for the doctor and pounds her fists into my mother's back. "You're hurting her!"

Deacon's stunned expression sets security in motion. Within seconds, four men grab my mother's four limbs and haul her away from the bed. She doesn't go down easy. She kicks and flails. Profanities ensue and curses follow. She promises to call the police and file kidnapping charges. And just before she turns the corner, she looks me straight in the eye and swears she'll see me at the church on Saturday.

When her wails reach the hallway, I swing my trembling legs off the bed and resign myself to my misfortune. The Walsh Family has caused enough problems for one day.

The odds are against me. If I proposition Deacon, it will probably end in a horrible rejection that I'll carry for years to come. For the sake of my battered heart, I should leave well enough alone.

"I better go with her. Thanks again for everything." The words feel impossible to pronounce. By the time I utter the last one, hot tears fill my eyes, obscuring my vision and clenching my throat so tight I fear I'll do irreparable damage to my vocal cords. I steady myself and reach for the borrowed robe on the edge of the bed.

Deacon takes the robe out of my hands and tosses it out of my each. He then turns to his sister. "Do you think you can take her Aunt Lillian shopping? She'll know what Eve needs. Her mother refused to leave her clothes."

Rory nods and zips out of the room before he finishes the question.

His features soften and a tiny smile appears. I lift my eyes to his as he draws so near, I fear he'll see my nipples tighten through my nightgown.

"Are you sure? I don't want my father to cause you any trouble." I hug my chest, cradling my breasts to keep them from view.

"I'm not afraid of your father. Get in bed, Eve." He lifts the blankets and points to the mattress. "A member of my family injured you in my house. If you'd like to press charges, say the word and I'll have him arrested. For now, let me take care of you."

EIGHT

DEACON

"Samuel, call Father Ryan and cancel Saturday's ceremony. Tell him today is his lucky day." As soon as I clear the door, I strip off my sticky sweater and bark orders while we head towards my bedroom.

"Lucky day, sir?" Samuel straightens his glasses and continues to write, running to keep up with my long strides.

"Yes, Sam! Tell that old goat I'll grant him the money he wants for the new pews. Tell him he can choose the most expensive ones under one condition. He needs to close the church this afternoon for renovations. No Masses or services until further notice." Panting as I speak, I kick off my shoes and stagger across my bedroom towards the sliding door. Fresh air hits my face and my body slacks with relief. My sweaty skin prickles, but my cock stays hard as a fucking rock.

Goddamn, it took every ounce of strength I had not to reach out and touch her nipples. I'm surprised she could understand a word I said with so much saliva in my mouth.

"Are you all right, sir?" Samuel buttons his sweater and catches up on his notes.

"Did you get it all?" I reach for a glass of water and unbuckle my belt. My jeans cling to my legs with perspiration. I feel like I just ran a marathon.

"Sir, what about the other churches?" He points his pencil in my direction, then taps his notebook.

"Good thinking. Send donations to everyone. Big ones, Sam. And each one contingent on them closing for the next week. I need time and I need to cover my bases. Get the synagogue too. It should be impossible, but I put nothing past Evander." I yank my phone off my dresser and beg Rory to make a pit stop at my safe deposit box in town. She's the only one I trust to get what I need.

"Do you know what today is, Sam?" I pull down my jeans and toss them in the hamper.

"What, sir?" He hands me a towel and returns to his notes.

"Today, I become the person I was born to be. No more bullshit, Sam. My father was right. I can't escape my destiny. He left me in charge of this family and today, everyone finds out exactly what that means." I lift my arm to make my point and cringe at the smell of my armpits. "Oh Jesus, I need a shower. I'm sorry, Sam, you'll need to yell at me from the bathroom. I stink."

"It's about damn time, sir. Can I put your brother at the top of the list?" He calls out from the vanity area.

"Cancel his credit cards effective immediately. Leave him his bank account, but no more deposits. He'll go on a strict allowance, and he'll start working for it. Call Sterling's mother in Toronto. He's wanted to see her for years, and Hugh's kept her out of his life. Fly her here as soon as she can make it. Or better yet, fly him there. Call a moving company and get a team into Hugh's house within the hour. I want an inventory of any family heirloom in his possession

— art, jewels, and valuable furniture. Everything gets returned today." I lather up and think of Eve sleeping peacefully a few rooms away. This is where she's supposed to be. She's not safe with her parents, and I won't let her live in fear.

Something happened to me last night. In the blink of an eye, everything made sense. My father gave me the power to protect my family the way he protected his. The way he protected my mother and their children.

His priority was always *his* family. And while I've been so concerned about not turning into my father, I've neglected having my own. I've pined for Evie from afar and nearly surrendered the love of my life to someone as horrible as Sterling.

I'm an idiot.

Lilian told me her parents planned to leave her destitute if she refused to marry Sterling. They kept her penniless and terrorized her into submission. I'll never let that happen again. When she's my wife and the Queen of Hampstead, her parents will fear her.

"Call my executive staff and put them to work. Have them call every Gallagher with ties to the family. Call every important family in town. I'm cancelling the wedding. Anyone seen offering sympathies to Hugh, Sterling or the Walsh family will become *persona non grata* and barred from any financial assistance or social events. Make it clear, Sam." I bang on the shower wall while I rinse.

"Got it, sir. I'll bust balls."

"Bust them good, Sam. Channel all the frustration these people have given us over the last fifteen years and plan to go ape-shit for the next forty-eight hours. If they thought my father was bad, just wait until they get a load of me." I wrap a towel around my waist and step out of the shower.

"I just got chills, sir." He shows me his arm.

"Me too." I show him mine. "I'm in love with Eve, Sam."

"That's old news, sir." He huffs and continues to write. "You always forget to close the tabs on her social media pages before shutting down your laptop. You've got a file on your desktop entitled Evie. And there's that photo in your desk drawer. Should I continue?"

"That's enough, smartass."

NINE

EVE

There's no way to do this delicately. It just isn't done. There are rules and I'm about to break a doozy.

How do you proposition a man for sex?

This wasn't God's intention. I'll bet this wasn't the chance he didn't want me to waste. But I thought it through in the bathtub, and I can't back out. I'm here for a reason and I can't blow it.

In two days, I marry Sterling. My mother promised she'd see me at church and she always comes through. Deacon can hold my parents off for a day, but I doubt he'll hold them off forever.

I've never felt so powerless.

Maybe this isn't only about sex. Maybe this is a way of taking my power back. Perhaps it's one last feminist statement.

I'll rise against the patriarchy with wet hot, sticky sex.

And I won't make excuses. I've got an itch that only Deacon Gallagher can scratch. I'm twenty-one years old and it's now or never. The only man I've ever loved is a few rooms away. What's the worst that can happen? It's a yes or no question. *Right?*

So what's my line? How do I break the ice?

"Deacon...do you like flowers?"

Flowers? I can't start like that. He'll assume I mean roses or violets. It's completely out of context. Besides, that sounds like something Zelda would say.

"I have a proposition for you." Proposition? No, that sounds transactional, like I plan to charge him afterwards. Where's the romance? Where's the sexy words to entice him into betraying his nephew?

Oh God, I hadn't thought about it like that. I know he's not crazy about Sterling, but he's an honorable guy. It's possible he may not want to sleep with the woman set to marry his brother's son.

And what the hell do I have to lure him? A borrowed slip and a robe? I'm not even wearing panties. *Is that a plus or a minus?*

I suppose I could attempt bold honesty. A man like Deacon might appreciate a few words spoken with an open heart. But what's my truth, and how do I keep from sounding insane?

Zara says all men like being admired. They can't help it. It's in their DNA. But I've loved Deacon so long he may think a roll in the proverbial hay will make me grow too attached and clingy. He may not want to risk creating a future stalker.

"Evie? May I come in?" The sound of Deacon's silvery voice sends a chill down my spine. It's showtime. I race across the room and check my reflection in the mirror. He's here and I can't put this off any longer. For all I know, my parents might be on their way with the police. I have one shot to get this right.

"Just a second, I'll be right there." I reach for the knob, then take a pause. I've ditched the slip and spent the last ten minutes seductively untying my robe and letting it fall from my naked body. After my proposition, I'd like to offer the goods before he considers the moral implications. I don't claim to have a perfect body, but I think it's nice enough to stun him into choosing sex over loyalty to Sterling.

At least, I hope it is.

Should I say a prayer? No, that feels sacrilegious. I give myself a pat on the back and pull open the door.

"Please tell me you feel better." Deacon sweeps towards me like a long-lost friend. His soulful blue eyes melt my heart, and his warm smile makes it sing. Legions of butterflies hear the song and dance the Cha Cha in my tummy. My strength falters.

"Much better..." Before I summon the words, he takes my hand and leads me towards a miniature balcony on the opposite side of the bed, overlooking the bay. I've been so distracted I never looked behind the heavy curtain. It's breathtaking. Everything about this house is breathtaking. And nothing beats the man in front of me.

How the hell can I ask him for sex? It's unseemly. He'll think I'm a floozy.

"I didn't realize your house was so close to the water. It must get so chilly here in the winter." I swallow hard and drown my poor conversation skills before he goes somewhere else. I've been sheltered for so long, I have no life experience to draw upon.

What do I say to a man like Deacon? *Should I thank him for saving me?* Yes, I can start there.

"I like the cold. You don't grow up in Massachusetts and expect warm weather." We're playing the weather game.

When you've got nothing to say, stick to the weather. Oh Jesus, I'll never get into his pants if I let this continue.

"Thank you for saving me..." I hold out my hand when he attempts to interrupt. "Let me finish." I take a deep breath and lift my gaze to his wide blue eyes. My heart pitter patters with every blink.

"And thank you for letting me stay here until the wedding. This last day is precious and your generosity means the world to me." When my eyes mist with the start of tears, I wave my hand back and forth across my face and pretend I'm on the verge of sneezing.

I can't appear weepy. Sad isn't sexy, and I want to be sexy for him.

Dear Lord, give me the strength to do this right.

Sweet Jesus, stop praying for help on how to sin. You're just begging for lightning to strike you on a sunny day.

"Are you okay?" Deacon waves his hand in front of my catatonic face.

I shake my head and turn back into the bedroom. He follows closely, nudging into my back when I pause abruptly.

"Eve, there's something I need to tell you." He places one hand on my shoulder and whispers into my hair.

This is it. I can feel it in my bones. *Just do it, Evie!* Screw propriety. To hell with morality and sin. You love this man. You love him with all your heart and soul. I know you want his love too, but you can't wait for that anymore. Time is up. This could be the biggest taste of love you will ever know. *Seize the fucking day!*

I spin around on the ball of my feet and nearly knock him down.

"Deacon!" My voice emerges louder than I expected.

"Eve!" He lunges forward and catches my arms. "Sweetheart, are you okay?"

"No, I'm not okay. Please, say nothing until I'm done. *Okay?* Let me get through what I need to say, or I'll never say it." I nod until he nods with me.

"Okay."

"Deacon, I love you. I've loved you so long, I don't remember when it started. In two days, my parents will force me to marry Sterling. They'll drag me down the aisle against my will. But I'll never love him. And just this once, I'd like to know what it feels like to make love. Because I waited for you. I saved myself for you." I lift my eyes to his and let my robe fall to the floor. "Will you make love to me... Deacon?"

He says nothing.

TEN

DEACON

IT'S A WELL-KEPT SECRET THAT MADNESS RUNS IN MY family. It's nothing too outrageous. No one ends up in the nuthouse, but some men in my family lean towards obsessions. Money. Gambling. Alcohol. Four out of five times, it's a woman.

I fooled myself into believing I'd escaped this affliction by denying the one thing I wanted most in the world. I've suppressed my all-consuming love for Eve because I knew it would bring me to my knees.

But love is power and something this big won't be contained.

Eve waited for me. This beautiful girl, standing before me, naked as the day she was born, loves me and saved herself for me. I don't know what to say, but I don't deserve such a gift.

She wants me to make love to her once. No, not once. Once could never be enough. A lifetime will never be enough.

My eyes rake over every inch of her milky skin. I skim over her legs, savor her curves, and get lost in the cleft between her thighs. My mouth waters and my fists clench tightly. There isn't enough room in my pants for the steel pipe impersonating my cock. I'm not sure what to say and I don't know where to begin. I want everything, all of her, right here, right now, every little morsel she offers.

"Deacon?" She crosses her arms to shield herself from view. I'm such a buffoon. I'm so busy ogling her, I've let minutes pass without saying a word.

I leap forward, snake my arm around her waist and seal my lips to hers. The taste of her kiss hits me like a drug. A bottomless obsession pulls me into an abyss of madness. I can hardly catch my breath. I'll never catch my breath. I'll live and breathe Evie for the rest of my life. This is my penance for loving a woman I don't deserve and I'll take it. As long as I have Eve, nothing else matters.

I heave her into my arms and carry her to bed. We land entwined, tangled in each other's arms, but I'm unable to pull away from our kiss. I feel like a fucking junkie. In seconds, I'm addicted to her taste. If her mouth tastes this good, then I won't stop until I feast on every inch of her body.

I scramble to my knees and pull my shirt over my head. Her green eyes grow wide and dark. She reaches across the bed to pull the bedsheet over her thighs. Her bare pussy comes into focus and I angle my head to get a closer look. She's so wet, I can see it glistening from all the way up here. I drag the sheet away and unbuckle my belt. "Don't cover yourself. I'm about to see everything up close, darling."

"Deacon..." She covers her flushed face but forgets to hide her smile. *What a naughty girl.*

"Don't you Deacon me. You asked for this, little girl." I jump off the bed, strip off my jeans, then crawl over her body. I lick my way up her thighs and stop to relish the steep slope of her waist. On my way to her breasts, my hand lingers on her abdomen and I imagine the smooth curve of what might be. If she's willing, I want to start right away. I want to fill this house with the sound of children.

I reach her breasts and devour the swell of each mound, feasting on their magnificence and branding them mine forever. I cup them both, admiring and squeezing her supple flesh until my body slacks with euphoria.

"You don't know how much I wanted to touch you last night." I lick her taut nipples then cover each one with my mouth. She squirms, then moans for more. I tug them firmly, then suckle hard until she arches her back and runs her fingers through my hair. The scent of her skin surrounds me and visions of days we've lost come back to haunt me.

I won't lose one more.

"I want you, Eve. I've wanted you for years." I run my hand through her wet slit and let her watch me lick my fingers clean. Like a wild animal stalking its prey, my mind buzzes with hunger. Nothing but Eve will ever slake my ravenous appetite again. She's everything I never knew I always wanted. I don't think I realized just how miserable I've been.

Her eyes widen with shock. "Years?" I trail a finger down her wet slit and stroke her clit until her thighs fall open. Her breath hitches, but she speaks through labored pants. "Why didn't you say anything?"

"You were too young, sweetheart. I'm glad you didn't see the erection you gave me when I crowned you Homecoming Queen. You don't know how much I wanted to tear that pink sequined gown off your body, spread your legs and make you come with my tongue." I'm shocked to hear those words come out of my mouth, but not shocked enough to remove my finger from her clit.

She shudders, then grinds into my hand. "I chose that dress for you." Her breathy sigh makes my pulse spike out of control. I sink my teeth into my bottom lip until I taste blood, then stroke harder. Her legs spread wider, and the sweet sound of high-pitched moans fill the room.

I haven't had sex in over three years, not since the day I fell for Eve. I've thought about this day, this moment for so long, once I take her, I'm not sure I can go easy. There's something about her wide doe eyes, pouty lips, tight pink nipples and perfumed skin that brings out the animal in me. I feel like a fucking beast and the more I taste the more I lose my mind.

"You chose it for me?" I trace lazy circles around her sweet spot and watch her bring her pussy closer to my face. I can't take much more. My jittery hands claw her thighs and prepare to pounce.

"I wanted you to notice me, Deacon." The scent of her arousal catches my taste buds and my mouth waters like Niagara Falls.

"Well, it fucking worked, Eve." I slide my hands under the curve of her round ass and lift her pussy straight into my mouth. Her sweet taste awakens my senses. My stomach rumbles, like I've just seen the thickest, juiciest steak and I haven't eaten in weeks. Pre-cum spills from the head of my cock and my balls tighten, desperate for release. I'll need the strength of twenty men to make it to the end.

I run my tongue across the slick line of her pussy and trail it across her hard button. I lash it once, twice, seven times, until she screams my name and tells me what she wants.

She begs for slower until her toes curl over my shoulders

and she hums a song I don't recognize. When her song turns to gasps and squeaks, I lash her clit with lightning speed, and plunge my tongue deep into her dripping channel. I know she's close. One more stroke and she tumbles over the cliff, splashing my face with her juices.

My mouth falls open. She's so ripe, I need to take her now.

ELEVEN

EVE

I don't know how I'll ever walk away from something this wonderful. His kiss, his arms, and tongue are better than I ever imagined. He said he's wanted me for years.

What does that mean?

I won't dwell on it. *Not now.* This was always about one beautiful night, and I won't ruin it by envisioning more. He's the love of my life and tonight means everything to me. Whatever it turns out to be, it's enough. It has to be.

My heart beats so fast it sputters out of control. His eyes meet mine and he lifts his chiseled body off the mattress, wiping my release from his face. My cheeks catch fire. I'm not sure what happened, but I made a mess. I wasn't aware those things could happen.

I watch with bated breath as his masculine hands spread my thighs to make room for his hips. He's coming for me and I've never been more ready for anything in my life. The only man I'll ever love is minutes from making love to me. If I don't steady my breath, I might hyperventilate and black out.

"You're so beautiful, Evie. You take my breath away." Deacon leans forward and lets the tips of his fingers graze my belly. My skin prickles and my lovesick gaze drifts from his handsome face to the ridges of his finely cut abdomen. His body is sheer perfection. But it doesn't end there. A slight bounce draws my eye to the incredible cock jutting out between his thighs and my mouth slacks. My belly coils with anticipation. *Or is that anxiety?* And why is this the first good look I've taken?

There's no time for fear or questions. Deacon pounces. His arms, torso and massive penis blanket me in warmth and soothe away my worries. Our lips meet again and we savor the taste of sex. My sex. I've showered this man with my scent and marked my territory for life. The filthy thought thrills me.

"I want you, Eve. Are you sure you want me?" His hand moves down the length of my body, lingers over my breast, then reaches between his legs. He holds his heavy cock near my entrance and dips it into my wet slit.

"You know I do." I curl one leg over his hip and throw my arms around his back. Of course, I want him. I've thrown myself at his feet and begged him to make love to me.

Our eyes lock and a sweet smile forms on his full lips. My broken heart heals and bursts with love. I'll treasure this moment forever.

"Let me make you feel good, Evie. Give me time to do this right." I hold my breath and feel the weight of his body encase me. While his soft lips distract me with a blistering kiss, his steely length invades me. Pain pierces my core and my legs tense around him.

"Relax, angel. This is mine now. I'll take such good care

of it." He sinks deeper, stretching my tight walls until he can't go any further. I release a breath with a loud shudder, and he pulses into me, pumping with tiny thrusts until I unclench my thighs and he pulls out.

"Deacon!" The pain startles me, but not as much as his absence.

He pulls out and thrusts back in. His mouth lands on mine and I lose myself in his kiss. We build a friction that tumbles into an ungodly rhythm we can't control. The harder he thrusts, the wetter I become and the louder I cry out for more. Deacon won't deny me, and I won't surrender a second in his arms. I can't. This is all I have. Whatever he wants to give, I'll take.

His stamina astounds me. He thrusts, then plunges and barrels in with such finesse, I beg for more through inaudible pants. My legs tremble. My raw throat can hardly form words, but I summon the strength to continue. One orgasm hits. I cry out like a banshee then tumbles into another. Waves of ecstasy drown me in sweat and tears and it's never enough.

"I've thought about this so long and I've saved up so much cum for you, Evie." His sweaty face and feral gaze frighten me.

"You don't mean...but what about..." I try to speak, but I'm too parched to finish the sentence.

His face contorts as his cock twitches inside me. "You wanted this cock, Evie. I'm giving you everything that comes with it." He drapes his body over my shuddering limbs and presses his lips to mine. It's my secret dream to have Deacon's baby. I'd never ask for something like that. I didn't think a man like him would want another man raising his children.

"No one has to know. I won't tell anyone, Deacon." I whisper tearful words as he finds his release and fills me to the brim with hot seed.

He thrusts until his body slacks, then falls into my arms. "No one has to know what, baby? What are you talking about?"

"I'm not on the pill. I thought you knew. If I get pregnant, no one has to know it's yours." I hold his gaze for less than a second before he snaps.

His blue eyes grow to twice their size and his upper lip curls with anger. "Everyone will know. Besides being my wife and having my name, I might just hang a sign from you that says *this is Deacon's baby*. How can you say something like that? Do you really think I'll let you marry Sterling? I called the wedding off before I walked into your room." He rolls to his side and curls me tightly into his arms, peppering my head with kisses.

"You did? Why didn't you say something? Deacon Gallagher, you let me throw myself at you. I stood butt naked in front of you and told you deep dark secrets." I crouch forward and reach for a blanket to cover my shame.

"You said not to interrupt you." He wrestles the blanket out of my hands and turns me to face him. "And by the time you finished, you were naked. I'm just a man, sweetheart. A ridiculous man who's loved you for years. I'm so sorry I put you through all this. Until we kissed last night, I never thought I had a chance with you."

I snuggle into his embrace and place my tear-stained cheek on his chest. The thump of his racing heart greets me and matches my own. I've never felt happier or safer than I do right now. What if my parents steal this away from me? "Deacon, my father won't give up. You know that."

He chuckles into my ear then kisses my forehead. "Angel, your father hasn't met me, yet. Not the real me. But he's about to."

TWELVE

DEACON

What kind of bullshit line is that? I can't see my face, but it's hot to the touch and I'll bet the farm it looks like someone slapped the shit out of me.

Because that's what I deserve.

I've lost my mind. Clearly, my love for Evie has turned me into a raving lunatic who attempts to impregnate his lady without seeking prior permission. Or without so much as an engagement or words of love.

I turn to gaze my sleeping angel and cringe at the sweat-soaked hair plastered to her forehead. She deserves a medal for putting up with my sexual demands. I rode her hard and took out three years of sexual deprivation on her innocent body. My lady isn't leaving this room without a ring. And maybe I'll call up for a massage. She's earned it.

My phone vibrates again. It's still tucked in the back pocket of my jeans, on the far side of the bed. I'm certain it's Samuel or Rory, and I need to speak to both. Afraid to wake

Eve, I slide one leg off the bed and then shift my bare ass off, hoping to keep the mattress steady. Poor thing must be exhausted. If I didn't feel so happy, I'm sure I'd feel a bit more shame about my behavior. But one really offsets the other.

I rummage through my discarded clothes and yank my cell phone from my jeans. It's Samuel.

Your brother is here. Waiting. Furious.

Evander is on his way.

Rory dropped off your mother's engagement ring.

Eve's new clothes are waiting right outside her door.

I jump into my jeans and shrug on my shirt. There's no time to waste and I'm ready for the fight of my life. Last night was just the fuel I needed. Eve just became the center of my universe. Everything I do from this day forward prioritizes her, us and our family.

Eve agreed to marry me. I held her down in the heat of passion, but I'm certain she needed little convincing. In a few days, we'll marry. There's no sense in waiting. Evie's mine and I'm hers. This was always meant to be. And I'll be damned if anyone ever mistreats or terrorizes the woman I love again. Evie Walsh was everyone's pawn, a beautiful bird locked in a gilded cage. Eve Gallagher will sing as loud as she wants, and when she does, the earth will fucking tremble.

"Did something happen? Should I get up?" Eve stirs and tries to slip out of the covers. Her full breasts slide past the bed sheet and my hands instinctively reach for each supple mound. I clench my hands into fists and pull away. There's no time to indulge my urges.

"Sweetheart, go back to sleep." I tuck her into the covers, then run to the door to grab her new clothes. Samuel stands nearby. He hands me the bags and the red velvet box.

We give each a childish thumbs up and I tell him I'll be right out.

"I can't sleep all day, Deacon. My parents will probably stop by." She stretches her arms over her head and reveals those gorgeous breasts once again. I tuck the blanket under her body and place the red box on her chest.

"This ring belonged to my grandmother. My father's mother. My father gave it to my mother, who gave it to me when she died. Today, I give it to you. Will you marry me... Evelyn?" My throat clenches and I choke up on her name. "I love you, sweetheart."

Her tiny hand fidgets with the box as her bottom lip trembles. She bites down to keep it in place. When she cracks it open, the tremble curves into a tearful smile that melts my heart. She's a mess. I've left her a sweaty mess from hours of raunchy lovemaking, but she's the most beautiful thing I've ever seen. I take the ring and place it on her finger.

She nods and holds her hand to her chest. "Of course, I'll marry you. I love you, Deacon. I can't find all the words to tell you how much I love you."

I fall into her arms and kiss away her happy tears. When the smell of her skin makes my mouth water, I know I need to pull away and get to work. One more second and I'll stay here forever.

"Rest, sweetheart. Rory and Lillian brought you some clothes. Come down when you're ready and we'll talk about the wedding." I plant a kiss on her forehead and sprint out the door with a hard-on.

THIRTEEN

DEACON

"You can't cancel the wedding, Deacon. It's tomorrow." My brother spots me from a distance and charges towards me. He points, flailing his arms while we descend into the parlor. Evander arrived minutes ago, and I'd rather not repeat myself.

"Deacon! What's the meaning of this?" Evander holds a notice from St. Augustine's notifying all parishioners that the church will be closed until further notice. "I know you're behind this." He tosses the flyer at my feet.

I step on it and continue my stride towards the bar. I serve myself a whiskey neat to take the edge off and don't bother offering anyone anything. They'll be gone soon. I don't want them to grow comfortable.

"Guilty." I hold my hand up and laugh with Samuel. "Father Ryan will make an exception for my nuptials, of course. I'm paying for all his renovations."

"Your nuptials? Who the hell are you marrying? You sound just like Dad, Deacon." He slams his fists into an end table and tries to shame me. It's his usual line and it might have worked until today.

"Thank you, Hugh. And be careful with the furniture, you don't have the money to pay for that if you break it." I gesture to Sam, and he hands him the long list of changes taking place in his life. His face pales as his eyes skim down.

"Where's Evelyn? Her mother wants me to bring her home. There are still plenty of other churches, Deacon." Evander stands defiantly with his arms crossed at his chest.

Sam interjects on my behalf. "All denominations have taken a mandatory holiday for the next two weeks. And Sterling left for Toronto this morning. He's on an extended holiday with his mother."

I clap my hands once and rub them together. "All is well that ends well. Sterling missed his mother dearly. And Eve is no longer your concern, Evander. She's mine. We're engaged. We'll marry early next week."

His face lights up and my skin crawls. Before he offers his congratulations, I make Samuel see him to the door. "You're not invited, Evander. And don't think this will benefit you."

Eager to see my girl and famished from a night of sex, I jump in place, stretch and race up the stairs to grab Eve.

"You cancelled the wedding to steal Eve away from Sterling? You should be ashamed of yourself. She's too young for you." Hugh crumples his list and throws it at the back of my head.

When I turn to face him, he runs like a cockroach hiding from light. Typical. He can't afford to lose what little he has left.

MAYBE SHE'S TOO young for me. But what's too young? I'm not only in love with her---I like her. That's a big deal. That's what gets you through the hard times. She makes me smile, she warms my heart and instead of making me feel weak, she makes me feel like a fucking caveman.

She's the incarnation of sex but she's also fucking adorable.

After she scarfed down two waffles, two eggs plus both our hash browns, she ran to her room and changed into sneakers, assuming we'd go for a brisk walk instead of the leisurely romantic stroll I invited her for.

I don't know where she put so much food, but her appetite pleasantly surprised me. Women never eat in front of me. They think I'll find it unfeminine.

Since when does nourishment have a gender?

"Deacon! Do you sing?" She pirouettes in the sand, then scales a rock to get a better view of the beach. When she feels steady enough to stand, she kicks her feet and belts out the chorus of *Beyond the Sea* like a 1950s crooner. My heart flutters with love and a smile pulls at my lips as I gaze at the most beautiful girl in the world. My Evie.

It's more than her perfect exterior. *Evie glows.* She shines brighter than the sun. No matter what life throws at her, she finds a song to sing, a tune to dance and fights to find a few sparks of good.

Her wind-swept hair falls over her face as giggles echo all around her. Her joy is tangible and her smile contagious. The sparkle in her eye would melt the iciest heart and vanquish the strongest will. I want to bottle it up and keep it with me always.

"You've got incredible range. I can't carry a tune to save my life." I gaze up at her flawless face and she places her hands over her flushed cheeks.

"I bet you say that to all the girls, Mr. Gallagher." She gushes and takes a deep bow. When she stumbles on the jagged edge of the boulder, I panic.

"Please, be careful." I reach for her hand and gently help her off the rock. When I step closer, the wind lifts her skirt, and I get a generous peek of the pink-flowered panties she's wearing underneath. The sight keeps me enthralled, mesmerized to the point of delirium. I swallow hard and feel a tightening in my trousers.

We clasp hands, and the touch of her soft skin makes me break free from my trance. Like a child, she makes a whooping sound when she jumps into the sand, then chuckles at her immaturity. "Deacon?" Her soft voice brings my attention back to her.

"I feel chilled." She hugs her chest and rubs her arms to warm them. The innuendo misses me at first. I wrap my arm around her shoulders and pull her to me.

"Maybe we should go inside." I keep her hand firmly in mine and set our course for the garden. She stays silent, but I spot her lips move, murmuring quietly without making a sound. "What is it, darling?"

She anchors her weight in the sand and spins me around, dragging me to the far side of the boulder. She releases my hand and positions herself directly in my path. Her expression alters. She looks serious. Is she angry?

"I said, I'm chilled, Mr. Gallagher." She angles her leg and slowly lifts the hem of her short skirt. "And you said this was a private beach. Isn't there some other way you can warm me up?"

My heart pounds violently in my chest. My mouth gapes to the sand. "Miss Walsh, I believe I created a monster."

She hops in place, happy she's gotten her point across

and oblivious to the madman she's unchained. I place my hands on her waist and pull her gently into my arms. Her hands fall on my chest and keep her steady on our shaky foundation. We kiss like newfound lovers, gently relishing every lick and nibble while our tongues explore and taste the sweet breath of our beloved. I'm so in love with her. I'll move mountains to protect her.

But when she asks for it dirty, that's exactly what she's going to get. I spin her around, clasp her wrists and slam them down on the boulder.

"Deacon, what the…" Her head shakes with confusion.

It's not easy to do everything with one free hand, but Evie makes me a better man. With one hand holding hers and hers sealed to the rock, I bend her forward and tear off those pink-flowered panties.

"Deacon! I just ripped the tags on those. I love them!" She whines but wiggles her ass into my hips.

"Do you love this more?" I slide my shaft into her hot pussy and grunt when her vise-like grip sucks me in. The sensation blows my mind. I fall forward, release her hands and grasp her waist for purchase. "Well, do you?"

"Fuck, yes!" Her honey-brown hair blows wildly in the wind, and her dripping sex bangs feverishly into my cock. My sweet, innocent girl gives as good as she gets. She's one in a million. Her hands, graced with my mother's ring, cling to the rock. I love knowing she's mine. We can be as filthy as we want. Our love is sacred. I insist we do this into our eighties.

The pressure quickly reaches a boiling point. When her moans create a sonata of sexual mischief loud enough to scare the fish and her knees buckle, I know she's tipped over the edge. "Where do you want it, baby?"

"You know where I want it!" She screams and loses her

balance, falling into the side of the boulder. It makes no difference. I catch her trembling body and finish the job. She wanted cock and she knows exactly what comes with it.

"Do you feel warmer now, baby?" I laugh and help her to her feet. Her bright green eyes sparkle as she dusts off her skirt and shakes the sand off her sneakers.

Her nose crinkles when a smile takes up half her face. "No, but I'm so much happier."

FOURTEEN

EPILOGUE-9 YEARS LATER
EVE

"Did you order the whiskey he likes?" I wipe my sweaty brow and chug the rest of my water while I race up the stairs. Samuel follows at my heels, checking items off my long list for Deacon's fiftieth birthday party.

"I did. Ten cases." He taps his notebook with confidence.

"The Irish one? Not the one from Scotland?" I stare and wait for confirmation.

He quirks an eyebrow. I've offended him. He knows this stuff better than me. "The Irish one, ma'am."

"Please, forgive me. I'm a mess. Deacon's not taking the big 5-0 very well. He's brooding night and day about his long-lost youth and the gray in his beard, which I think is smoking hot." I tap my sneaker on the freshly polished floor, then bend down to wipe the smudge. I hate making a mess for the maids.

"No, he's not. He went on a tirade this morning, demoted Hugh again, then cancelled his trip to London next week." He shakes his head, then returns to his notes. "And I can't get him to choose a band for the party. I know he's depressed, but I needed to book them yesterday."

"Demoted again? For crying out loud, he'll be a parking attendant soon. Let me talk to him about the music. Thanks for everything." I spin into the nursery and check on the baby. She isn't a baby anymore. Calliope turned one earlier this year. But she's our baby and probably the last one we'll have.

"How's Mama's munchkin?" I lift her into my arms and dance an Irish jig to a song in my head. Her black hair and soulful blue eyes make her look like a miniature version of Deacon... only prettier... and softer... and oh, so sweeter. I bring her tummy to my lips and blow raspberries.

She giggles and waves her arms in appreciation, grateful for a few minutes of alone time with her mama. It never last long. At the sound of my voice, a thunderous clatter of tiny feet make their way down the hall. I stepped away for a ninety-minute spin class, and I suspect they convinced themselves I'd never return.

Owen, Rowan, and Phoebe dash through the nursery door at breakneck speed, skid into the carpet and holler for their mama. They're eight, six and four, old enough to know the difference between an inside and outside voice. Lucky for them, my Cali is a perfect angel and not easily rattled by loud noises.

I place my sweetheart in her crib and look down at the rugrats violating my nursery time. With a stern face, I bring my hands to my hips. "Did you eat your breakfast?"

I get three nods.

"Did you do your chore for the day? Not the one you want, but the one on the board?" I point a finger at each one and let it linger on Owen, the biggest offender.

Three nods.

"Did you pick out your clothes for our trip to Boston later today? Rowan needs to make a good impression for his girlfriend, Gabby Novello." I tease my eldest son, who hides his face in shame. When his siblings join in, I threaten to skip ice cream time.

"Okay, I need to check on Daddy. Where are my kisses?" I squat to their level and get bombarded with hugs and kisses from my crazy crew.

I find Deacon sitting on our bedroom balcony, snuggled in a warm bathrobe. He's such a baby. He doesn't look a day over forty-five and he's got the body of a man in his thirties---a hot man in his thirties. Ever since someone pointed out that he'll turn fifty before I turn thirty, he's suddenly taken stock of our age difference.

Why would a twenty-nine-year-old woman want to stay with a fifty-year-old man?

For heaven's sake, I turn thirty next month.

"Hey baby, how's that gorgeous man of mine?" I strut onto the balcony and wiggle my ass in his face. "Did you get to eat?"

He shakes his head. "I'm not hungry, doll. But I'll take some of that ass. If you don't mind having sex with an old man." He sighs and fishes for pity.

I don't bite. "Not at all. I think it's kind of hot."

He squints, but I'm not sure if he's intrigued or offended I've called him old. "Oh, you do?"

"I've got a surprise for my birthday boy. I wanted to save it for Friday night, but you've been such a pill, I'll give it to you now. Let me freshen up." I jump in the shower, lather up, rinse, towel off and rush into my closet. There's no sense in messing with panties. The dress barely fits, and he'll just tear them off.

I take my dress out from my secret hiding place. It's

fresh from the cleaners who got it straight from the seam-stress. I've tried to maintain my figure but let's be serious, it's twelve years and four babies later. Thanks to yoga and spin, I didn't need extra fabric, but Miss Fiona did an excellent job of giving me half an inch here and there.

The pink sequins have kept their luster. My homecoming sash only needed a retouch of glitter. Giggling while I work, I slink my legs in and squirm into the dress I once believed would win Deacon Gallagher's heart. I saved for months to buy it, and it was worth every penny.

"Hello, Mr. Gallagher." I sashay onto the balcony like a runway model and lean forward, lifting my cleavage over the edge.

"Hello, Miss Walsh..." His eyes flare and his lips part with surprise. He sits up and fights a smile I haven't seen in over a week.

"How do you like it?" I bat my lashes and crawl into his lap.

"Okay, I'm over it. Happy Birthday to me."

THANKS FOR READING.

READ EVIE'S Friend's Zelda's Story:
In Praise of Older Men today!

Do you love Billionaire Romances?

Try these titles:

Takeover

Filthy Rich

Filthy Love

Blindsided

Gilded Cage

Magic Man

Hostile Takeover

There She Goes

Agreeably Arranged

Bad Boy

Do you love Friends to Lovers?

Shut Up & Kiss Me

Unsuitable

Lucky Man

Marry Me

Do you love Mafia Romances?

Check out my BROOKLYN BAD BOYS

Love Interrupted

Love Unleashed

Love Revealed

BAD BOYS TURNED GOOD?

Check out SCOUNDRELS IN LOVE

Bad Professor

Bad Boss

Bad Boy

PHILLY BOYS FIND LOVE IN LOVE BITES

Love Hate

Love Nest

Love Match

And many more - find them HERE

Thanks for reading and I hope you come back again!

ABOUT THE AUTHOR

Matilda is a Texas girl in love with a Philly boy who loves to write dirty books about two people who trip into love and fumble their way into a Filthy, Funny, Happily Ever After.

I live in Austin, with my husband, two crazy Chihuahuas and an even crazier cat. And I spend most of my day writing dirty romance books about older men who fall in love with younger women and make fools of themselves trying to win their hearts.

If you love Dark Romance, you've come to the wrong place. I don't like dark heroes.

I like my hero to be successful, sweet, suave, sophisticated and kind--- and then I want him to lose all his composure and game when he meets the heroine. I want him to turn into a bumbling idiot when he spots the girl of his dreams and revert to a teenage boy in a man's body trying to win her.

I like my heroines to be witty, intelligent, and unshakeable---who could do just as well without a man—until the hero convinces her otherwise.

I write A LOT OF AGE GAP--because I LOVE AGE GAP ROMANCE. I've got no other excuse for it.

No matter what kind of story it is, my ladies are ADORED, and my endings are always Happily EVER AFTER, not HFN.

To receive a free ebook, join Matilda Martel's newsletter.

Please head to my website to learn what's in the final stages and will be coming out soon!

www.ingramcontent.com/pod-product-compliance
Lightning Source LLC
Chambersburg PA
CBHW061357160726
47995CB00001B/351